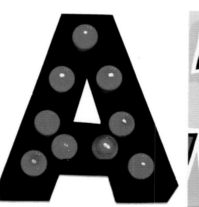

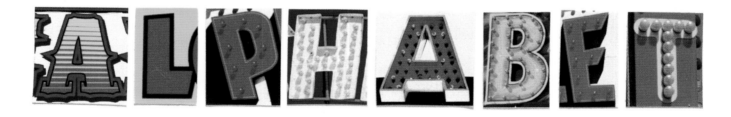

A FABULOUS FAIR ALPHABET

Debra Frasier

Beach Lane Books

New York London Toronto Sydney

JL Frasier

Special thanks to my editor, Allyn Johnston, for courage; Jim Henkel for invaluable photo smarts; Steve and Vicki Palmquist for computer patience and endless fair talk; Ian Hunter for life-saving dinners; and filmmaker Michael Hanisch for accompaniment.

And a "foot-long" thank-you to the workers at fairs everywhere—especially the Minnesota State Fair and the Texas State Fair (where I went in search of needed *J*s, *Q*s, and *X*s)—who create this annual celebration for all of us.

BEACH LANE BOOKS • An imprint of Simon & Schuster Children's Publishing Division • 1230 Avenue of the Americas, New York, New York 10020 • Copyright © 2010 by Debra Frasier • All rights reserved, including the right of reproduction in whole or in part in any form. • BEACH LANE BOOKS is a trademark of Simon & Schuster, Inc. • For information about special discounts for bulk purchases, please contact Simon & Schuster Special Sales at 1-866-506-1949 or business @simonandschuster.com. • The Simon & Schuster Speakers Bureau can bring authors to your live event. For more information or to book an event, contact the Simon & Schuster Speakers Bureau at 1-866-248-3049 or visit our website at www.simonspeakers.com. • Book design by Lauren Rille • The text for this book is set in Memphis. • The illustrations for this book are collages of Canson papers and photographs of letters that were printed on Epson matte paper. • Manufactured in China • 0410 SCP • 10 9 8 7 6 5 4 3 2 • Library of Congress Cataloging-in-Publication Data • Frasier, Debra. • A fabulous fair alphabet / Debra Frasier. — 1st ed. • p. cm. • Summary: Letters of the alphabet in various graphic styles accompany words associated with fairs. • ISBN 978-1-4169-9817-4 (hardcover) • [1. Alphabet. 2. Fairs—Fiction.] I. Title. • PZ7.F8654Fab 2010 • [E]—dc22 • 2009038329

For the inventors
of that most amazing of tools:
the alphabet . . .

  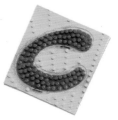

and for everyone
who makes our
fair days and nights
so unforgettable

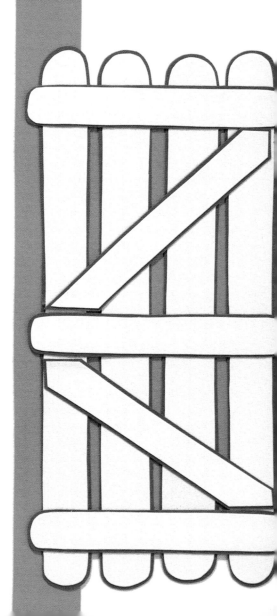

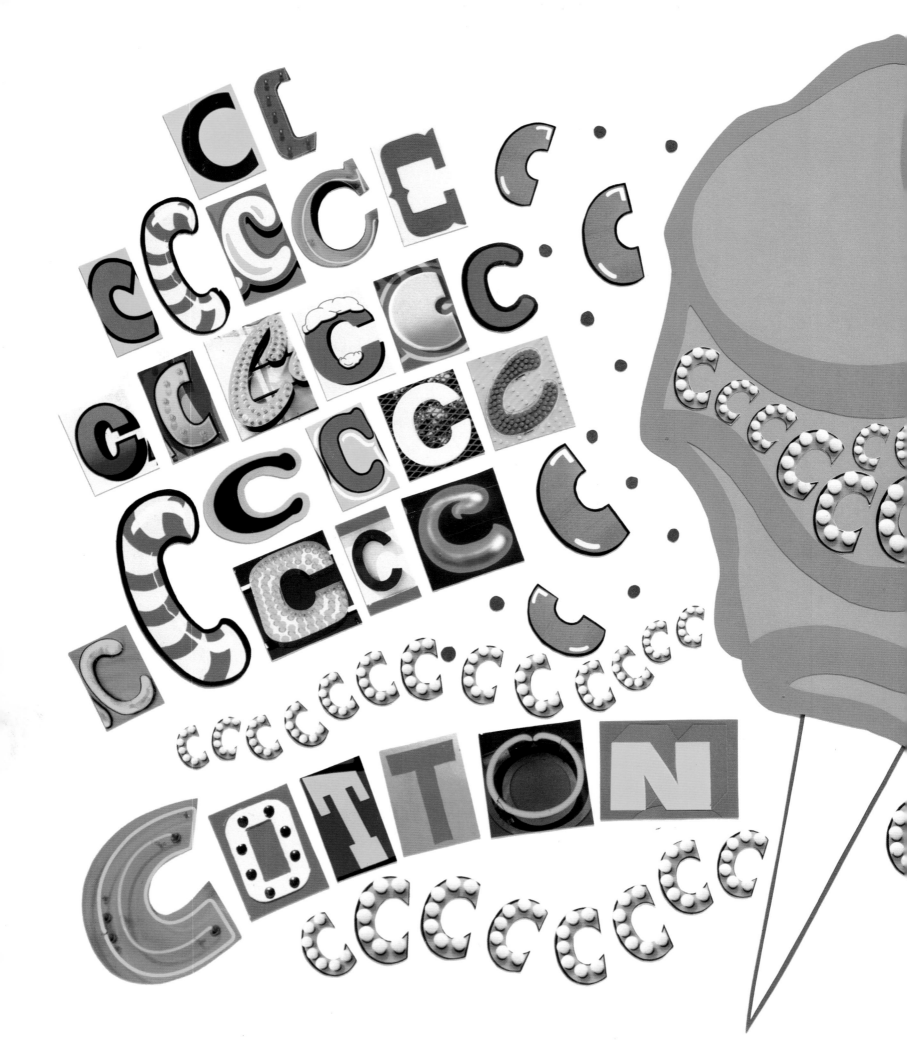

COTTON

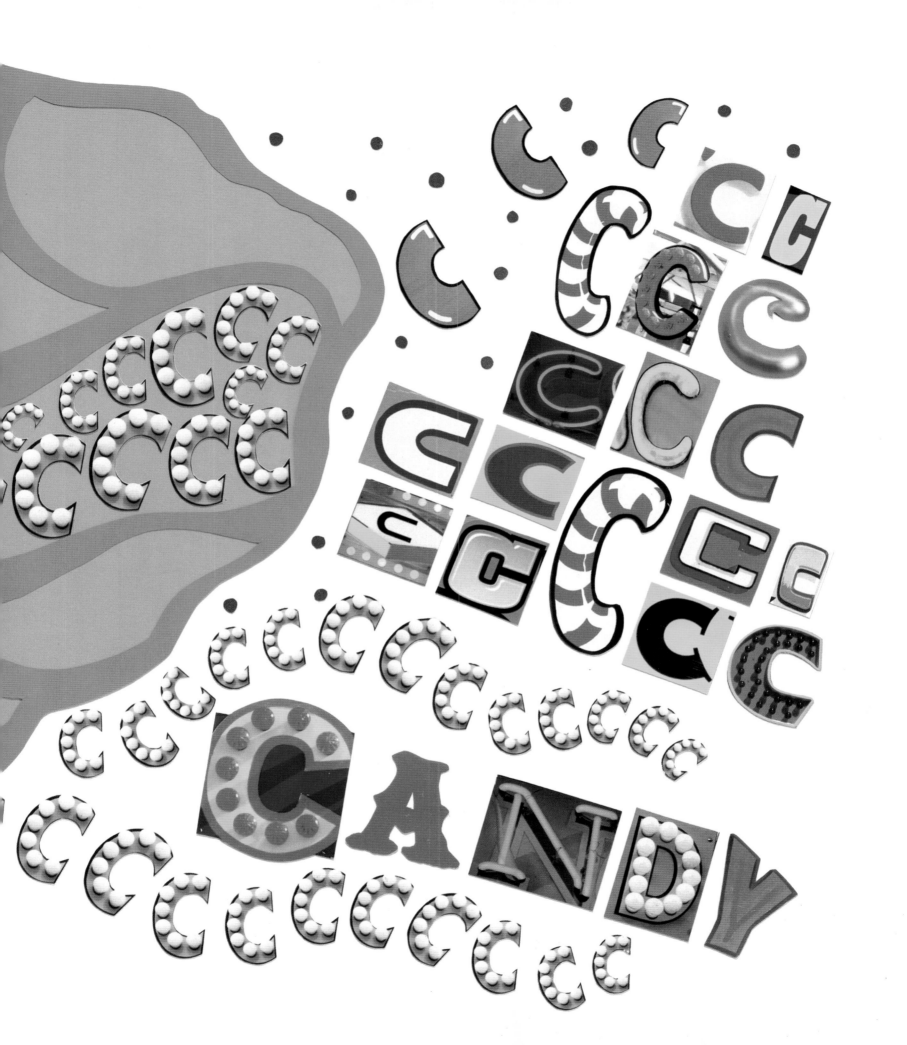

EAT EVERYTHING

FERRIS WHEEL

HOLSTEIN

ICE CREAM

JUDGING

LARGE

L L L L L L L L L L L L L L L

MiDWAY

PIGS

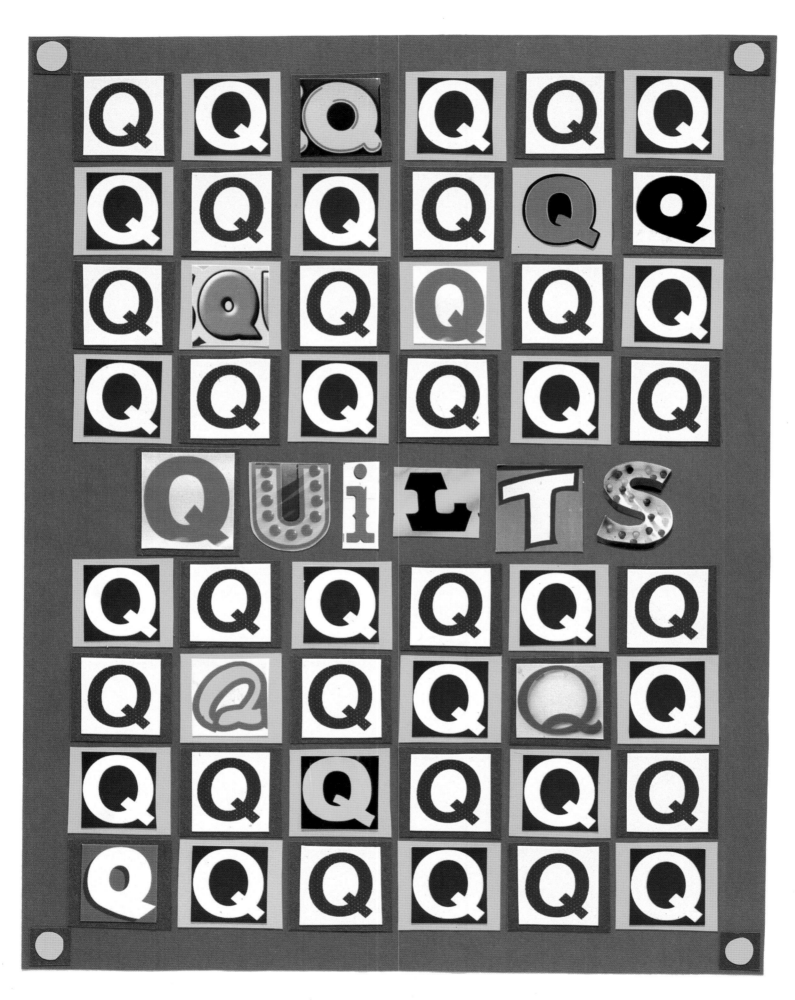

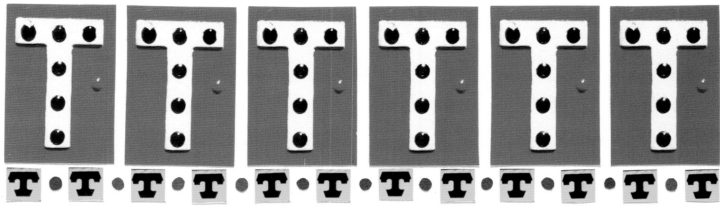

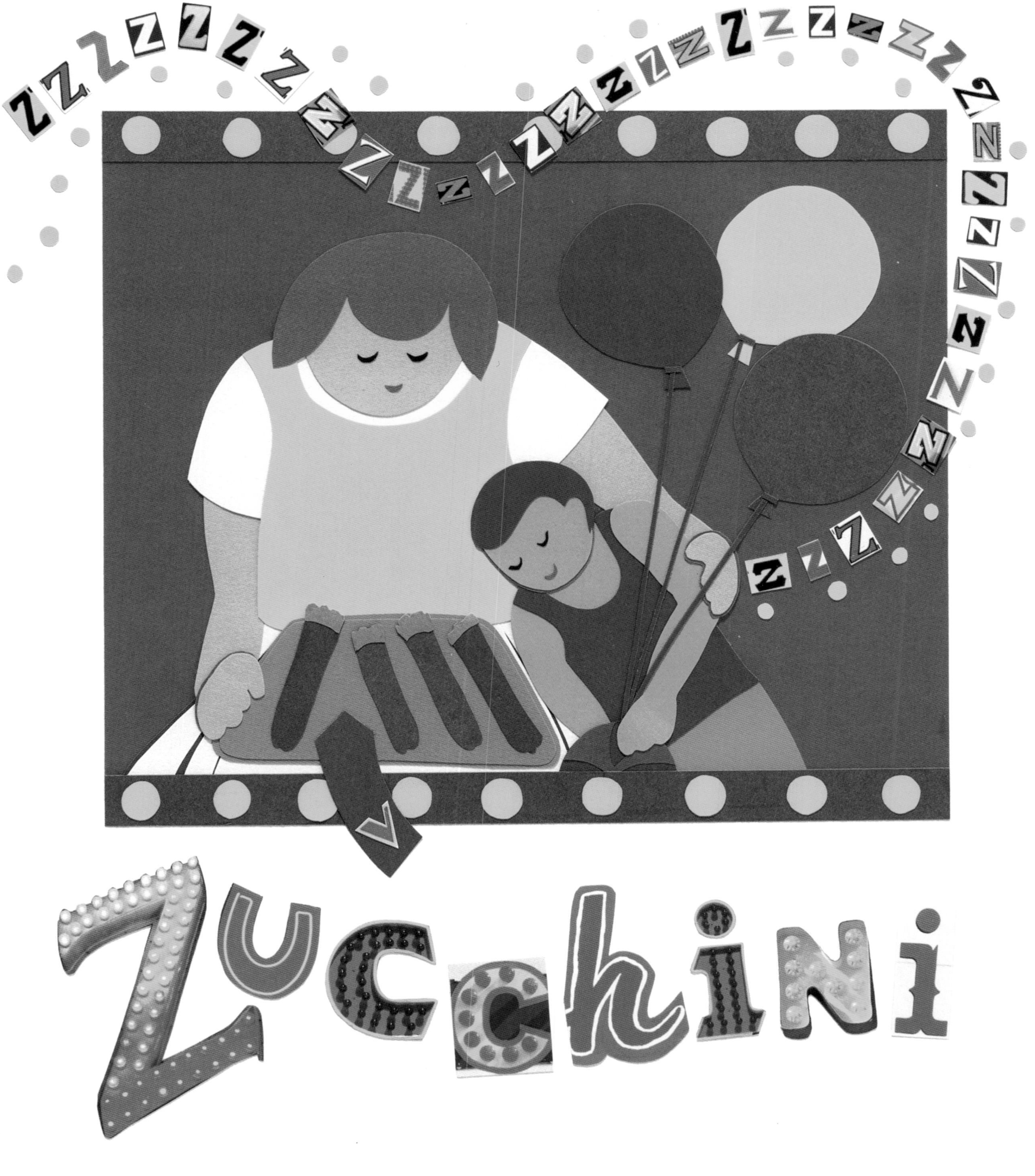
Zucchini

JUL 2 8 2010

OVEN *Fresh*

Ribbon FRENCH FRIES Curly
BBQ BAKED POTATO
Curly FRIES · Ribbon FRIES

Alpine Bobs

CANDY APPLES · CORN
COTTON CANDY
COTTON CANDY

DISCARD

NOPQRST

FUNNEL CAKES
ELEPHANT EARS | COLD DRINKS | We Make Our Dough Fresh

ROLL A BALL

TINY TIM DONUTS

Collection of eight (8) kinds of garden vegetables